AUTHOR'S NOTE

The Pueblo Indians of New Mexico and Arizona share a common ancestry, namely, the Ancestral Puebloans who lived in the Four Corners area roughly two thousand years ago. This story takes place in the early 1500s in the Rio Grande area of New Mexico, just before their first contact with Spanish explorers. *Pueblo* is the Spanish word for "village."

As they were before the Spanish arrived, the Pueblos of today are distinct communities, each with its own name, set of customs, stories, and sometimes language. I visited most of these Pueblos repeatedly for over ten years. Several families graciously invited me to their homes, their meals, and their conversations. We talked about many things— hopes for their children, complaints about neighbors, the joys of creating beautiful things. Sometimes I helped them prepare for their feast days, cooking and cleaning, or minding the store while they tended to other tasks.

When I was writing this story, I decided to tell of people that could have actually existed, rather than mythical figures from traditional tales. I tried to create characters that would reflect the warmth and humor of the people I knew. I tried to use cultural traits that might have been shared among many of the hundred plus Pueblos that existed pre-contact and which still could resonate today. Using the kind advice of my Pueblo friends, hopefully I have achieved some success in conveying the richness and vibrancy of their living cultures.

WHISPERS OF THE WOLF

Written and Illustrated by
Pauline Ts'o

Preface by
Vivian Arviso Deloria

Foreword by
Rosemary Lonewolf

Wisdom Tales

PREFACE

Whispers of the Wolf reminds us that young boys have always prized the company of an animal. A growing animal is grateful for loving care and in turn nurtures a boy into manhood. Among Pueblos and other Indians, traditions teach that respect exists between mankind and animals. Animals can truly help humans to know who they are and how to live in this world. In this timeless story, the author, Pauline Ts'o, tells of the devotion between Two Birds, a Pueblo Indian boy, and his rescued wolf pup who become inseparable companions. Both see the same sky, feel the warmth of the earth, are touched by soft breezes, and hear the cry of a hawk. They hold mutual respect for each other and for life.

—Vivian Arviso Deloria

Whispers of the Wolf
© 2015 Pauline Ts'o

Wisdom Tales is an imprint of World Wisdom, Inc.
Illustrations created with soft pastels on Canson Mi-Teintes pastel paper.

Library of Congress Cataloging-in-Publication Data
Ts'o, Pauline, 1961- author, illustrator.
Whispers of the wolf / written and illustrated by Pauline Ts'o ; foreword by Rosemary Lonewolf ; preface, Vivian Arviso Deloria.
pages cm
Summary: Over 500 years ago in the desert Southwest, a Pueblo Indian boy and his rescued wolf pup become inseparable companions.
Includes bibliographical references.
ISBN 978-1-937786-45-8 (hardcover : alk. paper) 1. Pueblo Indians--Southwest, New--Juvenile fiction.
[1. Pueblo Indians--Fiction. 2. Indians of North America--Southwest, New--Fiction. 3. Wolves--Fiction. 4. Human-animal relationships--Fiction. 5. Wildlife rescue--Fiction.] I. Title.
PZ7.1.T78Wh 2015   [E]--dc23   2015022016

Printed in China on acid-free paper.
Production Date: June 2015, Plant & Location: Printed by 1010 Printing International Ltd, Job/Batch #: TT15060109

For information address Wisdom Tales, P.O. Box 2682,
Bloomington, Indiana 47402-2682
www.wisdomtalespress.com

FOREWORD

When I first received the story of *Whispers of the Wolf*, I raced through this children's book eager to just read the tale of a boy and a wolf cub. I read it again later, to ascertain and reveal, although fictional, if it was a plausible depiction of a young Pueblo boy's life. I soon rediscovered my own world as viewed through the observant, respectful eyes of Pauline Ts'o.

Typing at my computer and looking out my office window, I could easily see Two Birds collecting the same wild medicinal herbs that flourish in my own yard here at Santa Clara Pueblo, in northern New Mexico. I was moved by Pauline's striking illustrations that imaginatively capture the dazzling palette of the Southwest landscape. I am happy to declare *Whispers of the Wolf* a satisfying blend of words and images descriptive of a young Pueblo boy's life—my nine-year-old grandson agrees with me!

—Rosemary Apple Blossom Lonewolf

Dedicated to the memory of
Lupe L. Romero (Taos).
And to my friends of
Taos, San Ildefonso, Santa Clara, Ohkay Owingeh, and Jemez,
whose support and encouragement
have sustained and nurtured this story.

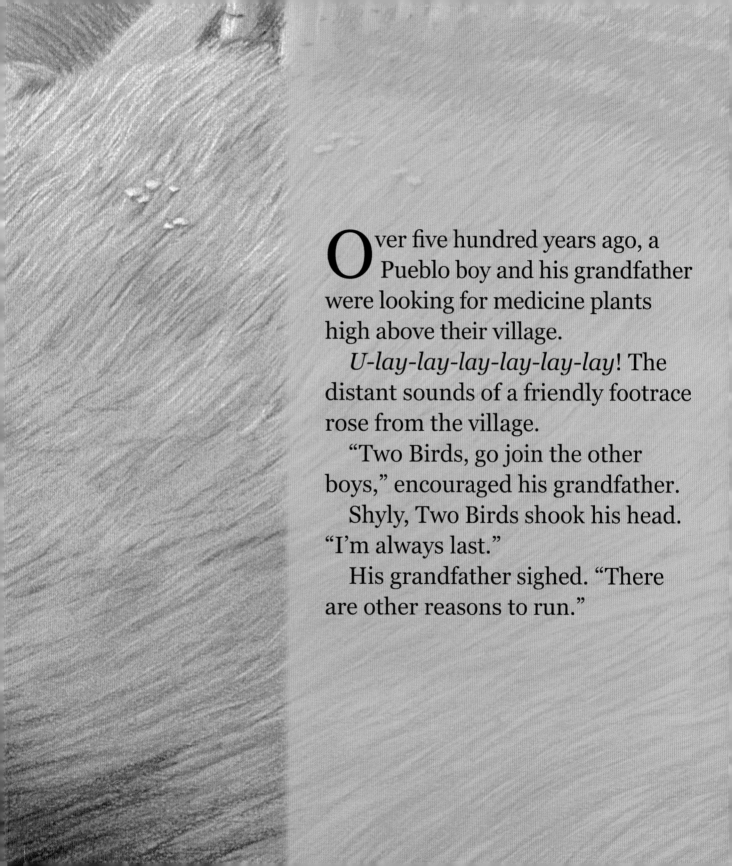

Over five hundred years ago, a Pueblo boy and his grandfather were looking for medicine plants high above their village.

U-lay-lay-lay-lay-lay-lay! The distant sounds of a friendly footrace rose from the village.

"Two Birds, go join the other boys," encouraged his grandfather.

Shyly, Two Birds shook his head. "I'm always last."

His grandfather sighed. "There are other reasons to run."

On their way home, Two Birds' sharp ears heard a whimper.

Auuuuu . . .

"Where?" said his grandfather.

Auuu auuu . . .

"There!" cried Two Birds. It was a tiny wolf pup. Too weak to get out of the hole, it barely moved as Two Birds lifted it.

"May I keep it?" Two Birds asked.

His grandfather said gently, "While the wolf spirit is powerful, this little one may not live long." But Two Birds was determined.

For days, Two Birds fed the pup sips of water and mashed-up meat. When the pup slept, he lay listening to the *pum, pum, pum* of its tiny heart.

One morning, he carried the unsteady pup outside.

"A wolf!" whooped Gray Bear, one of the village's fastest runners. "Where did you find it? Let's show the others! I . . ."

"No! It's not strong enough!" said Two Birds.

Two Birds was surprised by his own reply. Would the other boy be angry?

Gray Bear just grinned. "When it's ready, can I hold it?"

Relieved, Two Birds agreed. "Yes, I promise!"

Two Birds hunted every day for the mice and rabbits rustling in the grass. He gave them to his hungry pup and the wolf grew stronger. Soon, Two Birds let Gray Bear hold the pup, as promised.

"Can we hold it?" cried the other children.

Gray Bear turned to Two Birds, who stammered, "I-it's still too young."

"Pleeeeaase!"

But Gray Bear said, "*Shhh*. Listen to Two Birds. He knows his wolf. And I want to know how he catches so many rabbits!"

A smile spread across Two Birds' face.

From then on, Two Birds and Gray Bear hunted together. The wolf came too, once it was big enough. While they hunted, Gray Bear would often chatter about his brothers, sisters, aunts, and uncles. Two Birds listened and watched. But he also heard and saw many things the other boy missed.

One afternoon, the two boys and the wolf were resting under a lazy sky. Two Birds closed his eyes.

Whhhhhsshh . . . A soft breeze brushed his skin as his wolf's whiskers tickled his ear.

Two Birds heard Gray Bear ask, "What are you thinking about?"

"I feel the wind ruffle our fur and hear it speak of the lands from where it came. I hear the cry of the hawk as it carries rain to the mountains and canyons. I feel the warmth of the earth rise beneath our paws."

Two Birds stopped himself. He hadn't meant to say so much.

Gray Bear stared at him. "Where did that come from?"

Two Birds hesitated. "My wolf whispers to me."

"Why don't I hear what your wolf says?" asked Gray Bear.

"If you talked a little less, listened a little more, you might. And you might catch more rabbits, too!" laughed Two Birds.

But soon he was making up stories for Gray Bear—stories about what his wolf did that day or funny tales of how Coyote tried to out-trick Wolf. He even told about a swift runner who challenged all the animals to race. Of course, it was a wolf that finally beat him.

That day, Gray Bear said, "Run with us."

When Two Birds frowned, Gray Bear cheerfully added, "If you walked a little less, ran a little more, you'd get faster! Besides, it'll be good for your wolf."

Two Birds slowly nodded.

The next morning, Two Birds and his wolf ran with the others.

"*The sun is life!*" his wolf seemed to shout as it bounded alongside. "*Rain is life!*" And Two Birds could feel that every stride and every breath was a prayer to strengthen the sun and draw the rain clouds nearer. *This is why we run*, he realized.

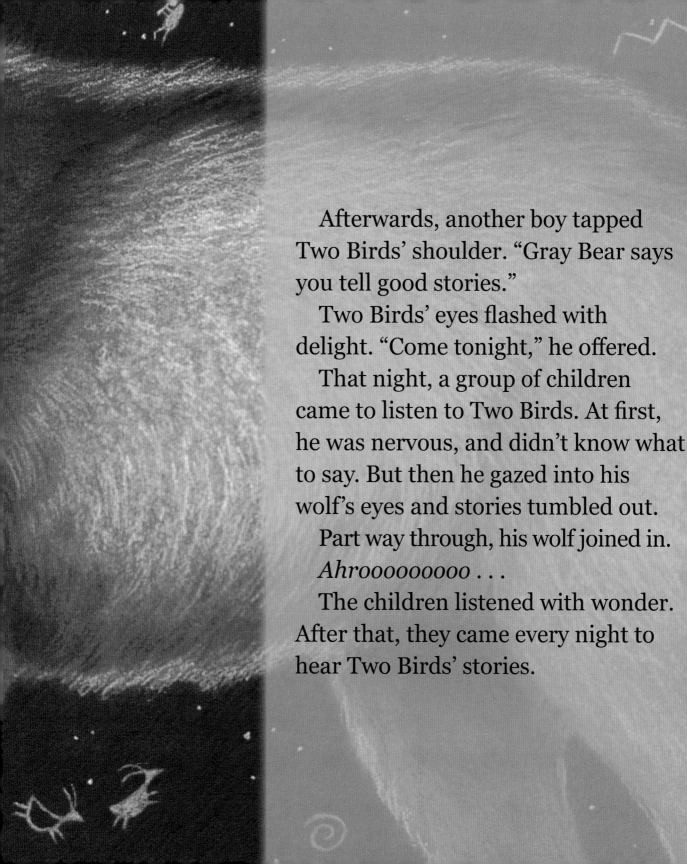

Afterwards, another boy tapped Two Birds' shoulder. "Gray Bear says you tell good stories."

Two Birds' eyes flashed with delight. "Come tonight," he offered.

That night, a group of children came to listen to Two Birds. At first, he was nervous, and didn't know what to say. But then he gazed into his wolf's eyes and stories tumbled out.

Part way through, his wolf joined in. *Ahrooooooooo . . .*

The children listened with wonder. After that, they came every night to hear Two Birds' stories.

Then one night, Two Birds dreamed he was a wolf, longing to run across the fields. But thick mud gripped his feet and he couldn't move.

When he awoke, he felt strangely sad. He pushed the feeling aside, hiding it behind his chores.

Summer soon turned to fall.

Then one night, Two Birds hurried to meet the others, when faintly—*ahroooooo*. Wolves. Wild ones.

Then behind him. *Ahrooooooo* . . .

His wolf.

This time, however, it sounded different. It sounded lonely.

Two Birds turned and saw his wolf straining at its rope.

He stroked the wolf's thick fur. The animal looked at
the boy with its brilliant eyes.

"*Did you save my life so that I would always be bound to you? Do you want a slave or a friend?*"

Two Birds wondered: "If I have no wolf, will Gray Bear still hunt with me? Who will still listen to my stories?"

But slowly, he untied the rope. The wolf leapt forward, stopped, and looked back.

"Go on," he told the wolf. "Be my eyes and
ears out there."
Then the wolf was gone.

Two Birds shivered and turned to find
Gray Bear watching.
    "My wolf is no longer mine," he said.
    His friend just smiled. "Come, the others
are waiting for your stories."

NOTES ON THE ILLUSTRATIONS

Pages 4-5 (*author's note / title page*):
Gray wolves used to live in most parts of North America, including the Southwest where the Pueblo people live. With the number of wolves rapidly decreasing, efforts began in the mid-1970s to preserve and expand the remaining wolf population. Today, wild wolves live again in New Mexico and Arizona and are protected there by the Endangered Species Act.

Pages 6-7 (*preface / copyright / foreword / dedication*):
For this story, I wanted to tell of people that could have actually existed, rather than mythical figures. I used traits that might have been shared among many of the hundred or more Southwestern Pueblos just before contact with Spanish explorers in the mid-1500s. But these Pueblos were, and are today, distinct communities—there are now nineteen in New Mexico—each with its own set of customs, stories, and sometimes language.

The tribal regions of North America, pre-1500, including the placement of the Pueblo people

Pages 8-9 (*Two Birds and grandfather*):
Pueblo extended families are usually quite large and close-knit, often living next-door to one another. Children are watched by all adults in the village, however. Acting up to gain attention is patiently, but strongly discouraged. Children who do not behave are gently nudged with words of explanation and by example onto the proper path—i.e., a path of contributing to community welfare and harmony.

Pages 10-11 (*pup in crevasse*):
Wolves give birth in the spring. Here Two Birds' pup is six weeks old, just weaned, and so is able to eat meat. Wolf pups grow rapidly, and by the time they are six months old, they look very much like adults. At two years old, they are fully grown.

Pages 12-13 (*Two Birds sleeping with pup*):
Pueblo houses are often built with thick walls of adobe. These walls, made from a mixture of mud and sand, absorb the sun's heat during the day and release it at night to create a fairly constant and comfortable temperature inside.

Pages 14-15 (*Two Birds on roof with Gray Bear*):
Pueblo houses often had no doors on the first floor. Ladders provided the only access to the upper levels. The roofs were often used as work areas and, in the autumn, as places to dry corn, strips of squash, pumpkin, and meat.

Pages 16-17 (*showing the others*):
Surviving in a land of little rainfall is hard, so group cooperation is essential. Everyone was expected to help out— for example, young children might chase crows from the cornfields, while boys would hunt for rabbits and other small prey with special rabbit clubs.

Pages 18-19 (*wolf whispers*):
Dogs were the only known companion animal among the pre-contact Pueblos and turkeys the only domesticated livestock. A wolf pet would have been unusual, but possible.

Pages 20-21 (*landscape*):
The Pueblo people primarily live in the desert Southwest around the upper Rio Grande River. Sagebrush, juniper, pinyon pine, and rabbit brush (or chamisa) are among the most common large plants surviving in this arid land. Thunderhead clouds carry the promise of rain.

Pages 22-23 (*Two Birds, Gray Bear, and wolf*):
With no written language, Pueblo beliefs and knowledge are passed along orally through stories. Tales about spiritual beliefs are told during the winter when the fields rest and the nights are long, while secular stories are allowed outside this period. As this story takes place during the summer, a budding storyteller like Two Birds would have focused on stories of the day-to-day.

Pages 24-25 (*boys running*):
A culture of footraces is shared by many native peoples of the Americas, especially before the coming of the horse, much less the automobile. Among the Pueblo people, running, like dancing, is an act of prayer, a way of communicating with the sun and rain spirits. Also, hunters might track deer day and night, running all the while. Sometimes, cornfields are 4-5 miles away from the village. Running to the fields means more time can be spent tending the crops. Thus, running is both a skill of survival and an act of the spirit.

Pages 26-27 (*Two Birds running with wolf*):
Wolves are known as strong runners. In the Southwest, wolves would mainly hunt elk and deer, but they would also eat rabbits, mice, ground squirrels, lizards, birds, bugs, and worms. Wolves would even add fruit and vegetables to their diet!

Pages 28-29 (*wolf and petroglyphs*):

Pictographs are images painted onto rocks, while petroglyphs are images chiseled or cut into rocks. Much of this rock art was created by the ancestors of the Southwest Pueblo people, who also created an impressive system of roads and Great Houses at places like Mesa Verde and Chaco Canyon. Some clearly depict specific events or mark special features of the area nearby, but the meaning of much of this rock art is unknown to us.

Pages 30-31 (*dream*):

The wolf was highly respected among the pre-contact Pueblo people. Depending on the specific village, the wolf is among the 4 or 6 directional guardians associated with north, south, east, and west (and above and below), along with the mountain lion, badger, and bear (and the eagle and mole). The wolf has important powers for healing, hunting, and war.

Pages 32-33 (*wolf moon shadow*):

The Pueblo people have their own names for the constellations. The Big Dipper is known as the "seven stars," "seven corners," or "seven tails" by various peoples. The name for Orion's Belt means "in a row" and the Milky Way is sometimes called "the backbone of the universe" or "white cloud like a road at night."

Pages 34-35 (*face-to-face*):

Wolves are wild animals with specific social rules. By the end of its second year, it would be natural for a wolf to challenge its pack leader, even if that pack leader is a person. As an adult, wolves eat 2.5 pounds of meat daily to survive and closer to 5-7 pounds to be able to have pups. In the wild, they travel 30-50 miles a day within a territory of 100-500 square miles.

Pages 36-37 (*letting go*):

Letting a captive adult wolf free almost always results in death, usually by starvation or by other wild animals. Young pups, however, are readily adopted by packs other than their own. Two Birds' wolf, which is only about 6 months old when released, would therefore have a reasonable chance of being accepted by a wild pack.

Page 38 (*wolves in the night sky*):

The tradition of storytelling lives on among today's Pueblo people. In 1964, a pottery maker, Helen Cordero, from the Pueblo of Cochiti made the first clay storyteller in honor of her grandfather. Today's Pueblo storytellers continue the art, in both oral and written form.

If you are interested in learning more about the Pueblo people, here are a few places to look:

- Cunningham, Kevin and Peter Benoit. *The Pueblo* (*A True Book series*). New York: Children's Press, 2011.
- Garcia, Emmett "Shkeme." *Sister Rabbit's Tricks*. Albuquerque: University of New Mexico Press, 2013.
- Nabokov, Frank. *Indian Running*. Santa Fe: Ancient City Press, 1981.
- Ortiz, Simon J. *The Good Rainbow Road*. Tucson: University of Arizona Press, 2010.
- Powell, Mary, ed. *Wolf Tales*. Santa Fe: Ancient City Press, 1992.
- Underhill, Ruth. *Life in the Pueblos*. Santa Fe: Ancient City Press, 1991.
- Yue, Charlotte and David Yue. *The Pueblo*. Boston: Houghton Mifflin Company, 1986.